Usborne First Stories
THREE LITTLE PIGS

Retold by Heather Amery
Illustrated by Stephen Cartwright

Language Consultant: Betty Root
Reading and Language Information Centre
University of Reading, England

There is a little yellow duck to find on every page.

Once upon a time, there was a Mother Pig who had three baby Pigs and they all lived in a tiny house. The baby Pigs grew and grew until, one day, Mother Pig said, "You're too big for my tiny house. It is time you had houses of your own."

Next day Mother Pig packed up a bundle of food for each little Pig and off they trotted down the road. "Goodbye, dear children," said Mother Pig. "Build your houses and, remember, never open the door to the Big, Bad Wolf. He would like to eat you."

Soon the first little Pig met a man with a huge bundle of straw. "Please, sir," said the little Pig, "will you give me some straw so I can build a little house of my own?" "Yes, I will," said the man and he gave the little Pig a big bundle.

The little Pig began to build his house of straw.
He worked very hard and, by the end of the day,
he had finished his lovely little house. It had
a big door at the front and a little door at the back,
and he was safe and snug inside.

The second little Pig trotted down the road and met
a man with a huge load of sticks. "Please, sir,"
he said, "will you give me some sticks so I can build
a house of my own?" "Why, of course," said the man
and he gave the little Pig lots of sticks.

All day the little Pig worked and worked.
When he had finished, he had a lovely little house
with strong walls, a roof and two doors. "This will
keep the Big, Bad Wolf out," he said, "and I will be
safe and snug inside."

The third little Pig trotted down the road and met
a man with a huge load of bricks. "Please, sir, will
you give me some bricks so I can build a little house
of my own?" said the Pig. "Certainly," said
the man and gave him lots of bricks.

For days the little Pig worked and worked.
He built the walls, put on the roof and fixed in the
windows. When he had finished, he had a lovely
little house with a chimney and two doors.
"I'm not afraid of the Big, Bad Wolf now," he said.

One day, the Wolf knocked on the door of the straw house. "Little Pig, let me in," he said, "or I'll huff and I'll puff and I'll blow your house down."

"No, I won't let you in," said the Pig. So the Wolf huffed and puffed and he blew the house down.

The little Pig ran all the way to the stick house.

But the Wolf came knocking on the door. "Little Pig, let me in," he said, "or I'll huff and I'll puff and I'll blow your house down." "No, we won't let you in," said the Pigs.

The Wolf huffed and puffed and blew the house down.

The two little Pigs ran all the way to the brick house.
But along came the Wolf and knocked on the door.
"Little Pig, let me in," he said, "or I'll huff and I'll
puff and I'll blow your house down."

"No, we won't let you in," said the Pigs. So the Wolf huffed and puffed and he puffed and huffed.

But he could not blow the house down. He was very hungry and very out of breath. He prowled round and round the house, looking for a way in.

Then the Wolf jumped up on to the roof and looked down the chimney. The three little Pigs quickly lit a big fire in the stove and put a huge pot full of water on it. "Now we're ready for the Big, Bad Wolf," they said.

The Wolf slid down the chimney and fell into the
pot of water with a big splash. One little Pig put the
lid on the pot and tucked in the Wolf's tail. "That's
the end of the Wolf," he said and the three little Pigs
danced with joy.

"Now we'll have supper," said the third little Pig,
"and you can both stay with me in my little brick
house for ever." After supper, the three little Pigs
went to bed, safe and snug, and happy that the Big
Bad Wolf would never frighten them again.

First published in 1987. Usborne Publishing Ltd, 83-85 Saffron Hill, London EC1N 8RT, England. © Usborne Publishing Ltd, 1987